Overall coordination: Susaeta Team
Editor: Ana Doblado
Selection, adaptation and preface: José Morán
Translation: Eleanor Pitt
Illustrations: Antonio Perera
Cover design: Virginia Martín
Picture design and layout: José de Haro

© SUSAETA EDICIONES, S.A. - Collective work
C/ Campezo, 13 - 28022 Madrid
Tel.: 91 3009100 - Fax: 91 3009118
www.susaeta.com

# Washington Irving

# Tales of the Alhambra

selection, adaptation and preface
## José Morán

susaeta

# Love and other treasures

Washington Irving (1783-1859), was perhaps the first American writer to be known across the globe. He was a passionate traveller who had a unique ability to capture the soul of the places he visited with tremendous sensitivity.

Following one of his trips, he published *Tales of the Alhambra* in 1832. This immortal work remains today the best literary guide to the customs of the spectacular Granada fortress.

The author, fascinated by the magic of Andalusia, reinvents the popular folktales that he heard first-hand from the locals, especially those from many moons gone by when the Moors ruled Spain. Tales which were narrated by the light of the moon or by the hearthside, during the colourful spontaneous gatherings that took place in the Plaza de los Aljibes, at the heart of the Alhambra.

Written at the height of the romantic era, the enthusiastic traveller tells tales of beautiful Moorish princesses, no less beautiful Christian captives, elderly Eastern sages, ambitious kings, miserable governors and bailiffs, heroic soldiers, enamoured pages, honest, modest workers and many other amazing characters. They all live out their individual destinies in the enchanted ambience of Muslim Granada, where the wonderful gardens, the whispering fountains, the chiming bells and the spell of its hidden treasures make everything possible.

There are two common themes in these stories: firstly, a love that can conquer all and that excludes no one; and secondly, the treasure, real and imaginary, left by the Moors as they fled Spain during the Reconquista. In their hasty departure they hid their fortunes, hoping to recover them when able to return to their beloved Granada.

With a style typical of the nineteenth century – charming, fresh, lyrical, witty and colourful – Irving enchants us with a wonderful literary work for all ages, considered by many as Granada's *One Thousand and One Nights*. It has stood the test of time, so the lucky reader will appreciate what a truly inexhaustible treasure he has come across.

# The Three Beautiful Princesses

**I**N TIMES GONE BY a Moorish King called Mohammed reigned in Granada. His vassals gave him the title *The Left-Handed,* as either through misfortune or lack of tact, he was always suffering from a multitude of setbacks.

One day Mohammed was riding along on horseback through the foothills of the Sierra Elvira with his large retinue of courtiers. Suddenly he stumbled upon a troop of cavalry, returning from a skirmish in the land of the Christians. They were leading a long train of mules laden with loot and held many prisoners of both sexes. One of those held captive was a beautiful young girl, dressed in fine clothes. She was weeping into a small palfrey, in spite of the entreaties made to her by a duenna who was travelling with her.

The King was struck by her beauty. He discovered that she was the daughter of the governor of a fortress they had sacked during the raid. And so he took her as the part he was owed of the loot.

The monarch fell more in love with her by the day, and decided to make her his wife. At first the young Christian rejected his advances, as he was a Moor and therefore the enemy of her people. Not only that, to make things worse he was getting on in years!

So Mohammed decided to endear himself to the duenna who was the young Christian girl's fellow prisoner, the modest Kadiga. As soon as the Moorish king started talking to her, he saw that she had a gift for persuasion, so he entrusted to her the task of winning over her young mistress.

"Why all this weeping and sadness?" Kadiga said to her mistress. "Isn't it better to be the sultana of this beautiful palace, with its decorative gardens and fountains, than to live the rest of your life locked up in that old tower on the border with your father? What does it matter that Mohammed is an infidel? You will marry him, not his religion. And he may be a little on the old side, but that means you'll soon be a widow and able to do as you please".

The shrewd Kadiga's arguments worked. The young Christian eventually agreed to be Mohammed's wife, and seemingly to convert to his religion as well. The clever duenna also agreed to be a fervent convert to Mohammed's religion.

Some time afterwards, the Moorish King became a father to three beautiful princesses, all born at the same time.

Following the customs of the Muslim caliphs, he called upon his astrologers to consult with them about such a fortunate turn of events. Once they had looked at their horoscopes, they told Mohammed that his daughters would need to be carefully guarded once they reached a marrying age. "When the time comes, keep them under your wings and don't trust anyone else with them", they advised him.

This triple birth was the only time the monarch became a father, as the queen did not have any more children. She died a few years later, leaving her gentle daughters to the care of her loving and faithful duenna, Kadiga.

There were many years to go until the princesses reached the dangerous age: the marrying age. "It would be a good idea all the same to take extra precautions", thought the wise monarch. And so he decided to shut them up in the royal castle of Salobreña, a sumptuous palace buried in the middle of a Moorish fortress on the top of a mountain, looking out over the Mediterranean.

There the princesses stayed, separated from the world but surrounded by everything they could ever possibly need. They could relax in lush gardens full of flowers and fruit, with aromatic trees and perfumed baths. In this luxurious abode, the three princesses grew into amazing beauties. They were called Zayda, Zorayda and Zorahayda, in order of age, as they were born at three minute intervals.

Zayda, the eldest, had an intrepid spirit, and always led her sisters in everything they did.

Zorayda was a fan of beauty and she would become entranced when she saw her own image in a mirror or in the crystal waters of a fountain.

Zorahayda, the youngest, was sweet, shy and extremely sensitive, always overflowing with tenderness.

And so the years went by.

The faithful Kadiga, to whom the princesses were entrusted, loyally fulfilled her duties as ward and served them with unwavering care.

Once, when the inquisitive Zayda was sat by one of the windows of a kind of pavilion inside the castle, she noticed a galley being rowed at a steady pace towards the shore. As it got closer, she realised that it was full of armed men. The galley dropped anchor at the foot of the tower and a group of Moorish soldiers came ashore with several Christian prisoners. Zayda told her sisters immediately and the three of them looked out carefully through the thick lattice work of the window, which prevented them from being seen.

Amongst the prisoners were three Spanish cavaliers, dressed in rich clothes. They were in the prime of their youth and looked as if they were noblemen. The princesses watched them with keen interest. Bearing in mind they had been living cooped up in the castle for so long, it was perhaps to be expected that the presence of these three handsome gentlemen, glowing with youth and masculine beauty, caused great emotion to stir in their hearts.

"Is there anything on Earth more noble than that gentleman dressed in crimson?" said Zayda. "Look how proudly he walks, as if all those around him were his slaves!"

"Look at the other one, dressed in blue!" exclaimed Zorayda. "How handsome! How elegant! How he carries himself!"

Gentle Zorahayda said nothing, but secretly preferred the gentleman dressed in green.

The princesses continued to watch until they lost sight of the prisoners. Then, with a sad sigh they turned round and looked at each other, and sat down on their ottomans, in a pensive and reflective mood.

The trusty Kadiga found them in this very same mood. They told her what they had seen, and even the duenna's weary old heart was moved.

17

"Poor young things!" she exclaimed. "Oh, my children, you have no idea of the lives these gentlemen lead in their home country. What jousting and tournaments they take part in! What respect they have for their ladies! How they know how to court and to serenade!"

Zayda's curiosity was piqued to the extreme. She asked incessant questions and did not tire of hearing the duenna's tales and lively anecdotes about her youth back in her country.

Eventually, the perceptive Kadiga realised the harm this was causing – she had three beautiful young girls of marrying age in front of her.

"It's time to warn the King", she thought. So she sent Mohammed a message.

"The time the astrologers warned me about has arrived", said the monarch to himself. "My daughters have reached the marrying age. What shall I do? They are hidden out of sight from men and are being looked after by the trusty Kadiga. Everything is working out well, but they are not under my care, as the astrologers told me they should be. I must gather them under my wings then, and not entrust them to anybody".

So saying, he ordered one of the towers in the Alhambra to be made ready for them as a dwelling. He set off with his guards for the fortress of Salobreña, to bring them there himself.

Ten years had passed since Mohammed had last seen his daughters. He could not believe his eyes when he saw the marvellous change which had occurred in them.

Mohammed prepared for his return to Granada, sending secret heralds on before him and giving orders for no one to use the road that his retinue would take. He commanded all doors and windows to be closed when the princesses were approaching. Once he had taken care of all of this, he set off with an escort of cavalry.

The princesses rode together with the King, covered in thick veils, on white palfreys. The horses were covered with silver bells, which jingled musically as they walked along.

The procession was getting close to Granada when on one of the banks of the river Genil a small corps of soldiers was spotted leading a convoy of prisoners. It was too late to get the men off the road, so the soldiers fell down with their faces to the ground, and ordered the captives to do the same.

The three handsome gentlemen whom the princesses had seen from the pavilion were travelling as prisoners in the convoy. They remained standing, observing the approaching retinue.

The monarch boiled with anger when he saw his orders were not being followed. Unsheathing his scimitar, he went towards them, ready to lunge at them with his left arm. The princesses surrounded him and begged him to take pity on the prisoners. Mohammed paused with his scimitar in mid-air as the captain of the guard knelt at his feet and said:

"Your Majesty, please don't do something which will cause a scandal in the whole realm. These are three valiant, noble Spanish knights who were captured on the battlefield, fighting like lions. They come from very noble families and we can get a very good ransom for them".

"Enough!" shouted the King. "I will pardon them their lives, but they shall be punished for their audacity. Take them to the Bermejas Towers and set them to the most arduous and difficult labour.

Mohammed, without realising it, was making a big mistake. In the midst of the turmoil and commotion of this dramatic scene, the three princesses lifted their veils, displaying their radiant beauty.

And as the King carried on talking, there was an opportunity for their beauty to wreak its havoc.

The hearts of the three men surrendered completely, their gratitude combining with their admiration of the girls. And the princesses were also more enamoured than ever by the fine bearing of these captives, inwardly rejoicing with all they had heard about their bravery and heritage.

The apartments where the princesses were to stay were as idyllic as one could possibly ever imagine: they lived in an impressive tower set apart from the main Alhambra palace, although it was connected to it by the fortress walls which surrounded the top of the hill.

The King thought the princesses would be delighted by the Alhambra. But to his great surprise, they began to languish and become melancholy. Nothing, not even the beautiful gardens, or the singing of the birds or music of the fountains, would cheer them up.

So the monarch called upon dressmakers, jewellers and artists from the Zacatín area of Granada. He plied the princesses with silk, brocade and dresses woven with gold and silver, Cashmere shawls, pearl and diamond necklaces, rings, bracelets and all kinds of other precious gems.

Despite all his efforts, nothing worked. The princesses continued to grow paler, sad figures amongst such luxury and magnificence. The King was at a loss.

"Kadiga", he said, "I want you to find out the secret ailment that is affecting the princesses, and how they can be brought back to health and happiness".

Kadiga promised to obey. She knew better than the princesses themselves what they were suffering from. She stayed with them in the tower and tried to gain their confidence.

"My dear children, what is the cause of such sadness and grieving in such wonderful surroundings? You have everything the heart could ever wish for!"

The princesses looked around the room with a melancholy air and breathed a sigh.

"What more do you want? Do you want me to get the famous black singer Casem to come along?"

"I'm terrified of the black slaves", said sweet Zorahayda. "And besides, I'm not interested in music anymore".

"Don't say that, dear child!" said the old lady slyly. "If you had heard the music I heard last night coming from those three Spanish gentlemen we bumped into on our journey.... But, children! Why are you blushing and looking so flustered?"

"It's nothing, dear mother, it's nothing! Carry on..."

"Well, as I walked past the Bermejas Towers last night, I saw the three gentlemen resting from their tough day at work. One of them was playing the guitar so gracefully... meanwhile the others were singing in turn with such panache that even the guards looked as if they were statues or were mesmerised."

"Couldn't you arrange for us to be able to see these fine gentlemen, mother?" asked Zayda.

"I think some music would liven us up a great deal", added Zorayda.

Timid Zorahayda said nothing, but threw her arms around Kadiga's neck.

What could she do? Although she was the King's most faithful servant, was it really worth destroying the hearts of these three precious creatures just for the sake of them hearing the guitar? Moreover, although she had spent such a long time living with the Moors and had changed her religion, doing the same as her former mistress, she was after all a Christian by birth. She had deeply buried beliefs at the bottom of her heart, and this is why she decided to find a way to please the princesses.

The Christian prisoners, held captive in the Bermejas Towers, were under the charge of a renegade called Hussein Baba, who was known for being very fond of money. Kadiga went to see him in private and, slipping a weighty golden coin into his hand, she said to him:

"Hussein Baba, my young mistresses, the three princesses who are shut up in the Princesses Tower, are bored and have nothing to amuse them. They want to hear the dulcet tones of the three Spanish gentlemen".

"What? Do you think I want my head to hang over the tower gate? Because that is the punishment I would get if the King found out".

"Do not be afraid. We can arrange things so that the princesses get what they want without their father finding out. You know the deep ravine at the foot of the tower – set the three Christians to work there and, when they are having a rest, let them sing and play as if it was for their own pleasure".

The good old lady ended her speech by dropping another golden coin into the renegade's rough hand.

Her eloquence was irresistible: the next day the three gentlemen prisoners were taken to work in the valley, next to the Princesses Tower. When the heat reached its peak at lunchtime, they sat on the grass and began to sing Spanish ballads to the melodious sound of the guitar.

The princesses listened from their mullioned window. Their duenna had taught them Spanish, and so they were completely captivated by the tender laments of the handsome minstrels. Wise Kadiga, however, pretended to be outraged.

"Allah save us!" she exclaimed. "So now these gentlemen are singing lovelorn ballads to you! Has one ever seen such cheek? I am going to go and speak to the foreman right now and tell him to beat them harshly!"

"Punish such charming gentlemen because they have a gift for singing so sweetly?"

The beautiful princesses were horrified at this cruel thought. The good duenna's righteous indignation was easily appeased. Also, it seemed as if the music had produced a positive effect on her mistresses, whose cheeks were starting to gradually colour, and whose fine eyes were lighting up again.

When the gentlemen stopped singing, the princesses stayed quiet for a brief moment. But then Zorayda picked up her lute and, with a quavering emotional voice, sung a little tune. The words were:

> *In its green bed*
> *Grows the hidden rose,*
> *Enjoying the sound of*
> *The nightingale's call*

From then on, the gentlemen were brought to work in the ravine nearly every day.

But after a while the Christian gentlemen suddenly stopped appearing in the valley. After a few days, the trusty Kadiga went out to find out what had happened and came back shortly after with a troubled look on her face.

"Oh, my dear children!" she cried. "Didn't I predict what would happen with all of this, but this is what you wished for! You can hang your lutes back up on the willows, as the Spanish gentlemen have had the ransom paid by their families. They are in Granada by now, arranging their return to their homeland.

The besotted princesses were completely desolate for the next two days.

On the third morning, Kadiga came into the room where they were sat, trembling with indignation.

"Who would have thought it! Well, I'd deserve to be had for treason against your father. Never mention those Christian gentlemen again!"

"But what has happened, dear Kadiga?" exclaimed the three princesses anxiously.

"What has happened? Well they have betrayed me, or they might as well have done so, as they have asked me to commit treason! Me, the most loyal and faithful of all vassals! Yes, my daughters, the Spanish gentlemen have dared to ask me to persuade you to run off with them to Cordoba, where they want to make you their wives".

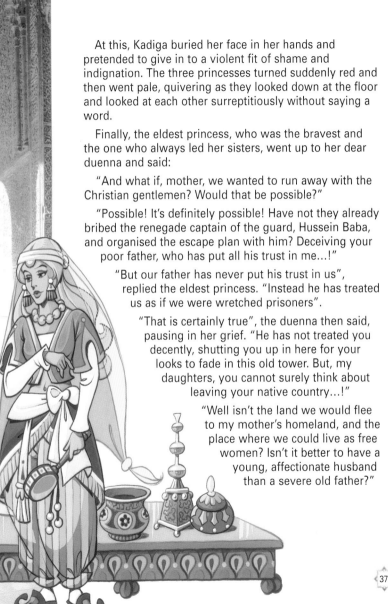

At this, Kadiga buried her face in her hands and pretended to give in to a violent fit of shame and indignation. The three princesses turned suddenly red and then went pale, quivering as they looked down at the floor and looked at each other surreptitiously without saying a word.

Finally, the eldest princess, who was the bravest and the one who always led her sisters, went up to her dear duenna and said:

"And what if, mother, we wanted to run away with the Christian gentlemen? Would that be possible?"

"Possible! It's definitely possible! Have not they already bribed the renegade captain of the guard, Hussein Baba, and organised the escape plan with him? Deceiving your poor father, who has put all his trust in me…!"

"But our father has never put his trust in us", replied the eldest princess. "Instead he has treated us as if we were wretched prisoners".

"That is certainly true", the duenna then said, pausing in her grief. "He has not treated you decently, shutting you up in here for your looks to fade in this old tower. But, my daughters, you cannot surely think about leaving your native country…!"

"Well isn't the land we would flee to my mother's homeland, and the place where we could live as free women? Isn't it better to have a young, affectionate husband than a severe old father?"

"Well, that is also all true! And I must admit your father is a bit of a tyrant. But think about it carefully my children! Would you be brave enough to give up your father's religion?"

"The religion of Christ was our mother's original faith", said the eldest princess. "I am willing to convert and sure that my sisters will follow my example".

"You are right, my dearest!" exclaimed the loving duenna, cheering up. "It was your mother's religion of birth, and on her dying bed she bitterly regretted having foresworn it. I promised to take care of your souls afterwards and now I am truly full of joy to see you on the road to salvation. Yes, dearest daughters, I was also born a Christian, and I have always continued to be one in the depths of my heart. I am determined to go back to my former faith".

In a word: it turns out the ever so trusty and clever duenna had gone to talk with the gentlemen and the renegade, and had decided upon the whole plan of escape.

The steep hill on which the Alhambra was built had endless underground passages leading from the fortress to various places in the city. It was through one of these passages that Hussein Baba planned to help the princesses out towards an exit beyond the city walls. There, the gentlemen had prepared some light steeds to flee rapidly with them over the border.

And so the appointed night arrived. The tower where the princesses lived was locked as usual and the Alhambra was bathed in a deep silence. At about midnight, Kadiga heard Hussein Baba from the mullioned window. He was down below and gave the signal. The duenna tied the end of a rope ladder to the window and let it drop into the garden. Then she climbed down it. The two eldest princesses followed her, their hearts beating fiercely.

When it was Zorahayda's turn, however, she hesitated and trembled. She tried several times to put her delicate, tiny foot on the ladder, and time and time again took it off, her troubled heart beating all the more wildly the longer she hesitated. It is impossible to describe the struggle taking place in the poor girl's breast... In spite of her sisters' pleas, she remained indecisive.

The risk of getting caught was getting greater every second. They heard steps in the distance. The unhappy Zorahayda fell prey to a feverish agitation and then, untying the rope ladder with desperate resolution, she let it drop from the window.

"Everything is over!" she exclaimed. "I can no longer flee! Let Allah guide you and bless you, my dear beloved sisters!"

The two elder princesses were horrified at the idea of leaving her behind, and would have preferred to stay. But the patrol was getting closer and they were hastily carried away to the underground passage. Outside of the grounds, the Spanish gentlemen were waiting for them, disguised as Moor soldiers from the guard the renegade was leading.

Zorahayda's lover was beside himself when he saw that she had refused to leave the tower, but there was no time to waste on useless regrets. The two princesses were raised up onto the back of their lovers' horses, and the trusty Kadiga mounted behind the renegade Hussein Baba. They all set off hurriedly towards the Pass of Lope, a path that winds through the mountains to Cordoba.

They had not gone very far when they heard the noise of drums and trumpets from the walls of the Alhambra. They raced as fast as they could, but as they galloped they saw that the light blazing from the Alhambra was being answered in all directions, with more and more lights appearing from the watchtowers in the mountains.

"Quick, quick!" shouted the renegade. "To the bridge, to the bridge, before the alarm is raised there!"

At the bridge tower, they could see lots of lights, and amongst them the glinting of soldiers' armour. The renegade signalled to the gentlemen and left the road, going alongside the river for a while and eventually plunging into it. They arrived at the shore on the other side and were guided by the renegade through the steep passes and rugged cliffs of the mountains.

And so they managed to reach the ancient city of Cordoba, where they were welcomed with great festivities. The princesses were received into the Church and, once they had fully adopted the holy Christian faith, they were married and lived happily ever after.

Little is known about how the monarch reacted when he found out his daughters had escaped. However, what we do know is that he was very careful to keep the daughter who remained, the unhappy one who had not had the courage to escape.

It is also thought that the princess secretly regretted having stayed behind in the tower. It is said that she is sometimes seen on top of the ramparts, looking out sadly at the mountains towards Cordoba. At times, you could hear her playing chords on her lute and singing heartfelt songs where she lamented the loss of her sisters and her lover, trying to console herself about her solitary existence.

She died young and, according to popular rumour, was laid to rest in a vault beneath the tower, her premature demise creating many a legend.

# The Arabian Astrologer

**M**ANY CENTURIES AGO, there was a Moorish king called Aben Habuz, who reigned over the kingdom of Granada. He was a retired warrior who, after a life of pillaging and fighting, was now weak and ailing, and longed simply to quietly enjoy the possessions he had seized from his neighbours.

However it happened that the ageing monarch at that time had to fight against some young princes, who were looking to settle some scores over the land he had seized from them. Finding himself surrounded by disgruntled subjects, he was at a disadvantage because of Granada's location, circled by wild mountains that enabled enemies to approach without being seen. The hapless Aben Habuz lived therefore in a permanent state of alarm, constantly on the lookout out for any imminent attacks.

Whilst all of this was going on, an old Arabian doctor arrived at the King's court. He had walked on a pilgrimage from Egypt to Granada, with the help only of an old staff he carried that was covered in hieroglyphics. His name was Ibrahim and he was thought to be a contemporary of Mohammed, as he was the son of Abu Ayub, the last companion of the Prophet.

For many years he lived in Egypt, where he mainly studied magic. It was said of him that he had discovered the secret of prolonging life, and so had reached the grand old age of over two hundred years. This peculiar old man was well received by the monarch, as he had begun to make doctors his favourites. He invited the astrologer to live in the palace, but the astrologer preferred to dwell in a cave on the edge of the hill where the Alhambra was located. Through a round hole in the roof, he was able to observe the skies both day and night.

The wise Ibrahim soon became the King's trusted adviser, whom he consulted whenever there appeared to be any trouble. Once, when Aben Habuz was complaining about the constant state of vigilance he had to be in to protect himself from invasion, the astrologer said to him:

"Know this, oh King! When I was in Egypt I saw a wonderful invention by an ancient pagan priest. On top of a mountain that looked over the city of Borsa, facing the great Nile valley, there was a bronze statue of a ram with a cockerel on top of it, turning on a pivot. Whenever the country was under threat from invasion, the ram would point in the direction of the enemy and the cockerel would crow, giving the inhabitants of the city time to defend themselves.

"God is great!" exclaimed the afflicted Aben Habuz. "What a blessing it would be for me to have a ram like that with a cockerel that crowed when danger was approaching!"

51

"Oh, King! I am a master of all the magical arts. I am so familiar with the mystery of the Borsa talisman that I could make one like it here, with even greater powers".

"Oh, wise son of Abu Ayub! I need that talisman. Give me such a safeguard and you shall have all the riches you like from my treasury".

The astrologer set straight to work to satisfy the monarch's wishes. He built a great tower on the highest point of the royal palace. There he prepared a circular room with windows looking over all the points of the quadrant. In front of each window he put a table upon which miniature small infantry and cavalry sets like those you find on a chessboard were arranged, and with the figure of the sovereign who ruled in that direction. All were carved from wood.

On each table there was also a small lance the size of a graver tool.

On top of the tower he placed a bronze figure that represented a Moor on horseback, turning on a pivot, with a shield on his arm and his lance raised. The horseman was looking towards the city, as if he were guarding it. But if any foe approached, the figure pointed in his direction and brandished his lance as if he were about to attack.

Once the talisman was finished, Aben Habuz could not wait to try out the ingenious invention. And his wishes soon came true, as one morning the sentinel who guarded the tower brought tidings that the bronze horseman was pointing towards the Elvira mountains, and the lance was pointing directly at the Pass of Lope.

"Let the trumpets and drums sound to arms, and all of Granada be on alert!" said Aben Habuz.

"Oh King!" replied the astrologer. "I do not need to use force to free you of your enemies. Send your attendants away and let's go alone up to the secret hall in the tower."

They went up the stairs and opened the bronze door to go inside. The window that overlooked the Pass of Lope was open.

"In that direction lies the danger", said the astrologer. "Come closer and look at the mystery of the table".

King Aben Habuz approached what looked like a chessboard with wooden figures. To his great surprise, he saw that they were all moving: the horses were in a fright and bucking wildly, the warriors were brandishing their weapons, and there was a faraway sound of drums and trumpets, the clashing of arms and the whinnying of steeds.

"Behold", said the astrologer, "the proof that your enemies are still in the field."

"If you want to spread panic and confusion amongst them, and get them to withdraw without shedding any blood, hit these figures with the tip of this magic lance; but if you want blood to be shed, injure them with the point."

The face of the peace-loving Aben Habuz turned pale and he hesitated as he came closer to the table, his beard trembling eagerly:

"Son of Abu Ayub, I think we shall see some blood spilled!" he exclaimed. And so he seized the magic lance and thrust it into some of the tiny figures, striking others with the tip. Some fell down on the table as if they were dead and the rest turned on each other, starting a fight.

It was hard for the astrologer to contain the monarch and prevent him from completely wiping out his enemies; at last he persuaded him to come down from the tower and send scouts out to the Pass of Lope.

The scouts came back bearing news that a Christian army had penetrated into the heart of the mountains, almost reaching Granada. There had been a disagreement between them and they had started fighting each other until, after a great deal of carnage, they withdrew to the border.

Aben Habuz was wild with joy at seeing how well the talisman worked.

"At last", he said, "I can enjoy a peaceful life and all my enemies will be in my power. Oh, wise son of Abu Ayub! What can I grant you as a reward for such a wonderful blessing?"

"The needs of an old man and a philosopher are few and simple, oh King! Grant me just the means to make my cave more habitable".

"How fine is the temperance of this true sage!" exclaimed Aben Habuz, secretly rejoicing that he asked for such a small reward. He ordered his treasurer to give Ibrahim whatever he needed to do up and furnish his cave.

The astrologer asked for further rooms to be carved out of the rock, and had them decorated and furnished with luxurious ottomans and divans, and the walls covered with rich silk tapestries from Damascus. He also had some baths built, filled with all kinds of scents and aromatic oils. At last, the apartments were finished, and formed a sumptuous underground palace.

"Now I am content", said Ibrahim Eben Abu Ayub to the treasurer. "I don't require anything else apart from a mere trifle to entertain me between my mental labours. I would love to have some dancing girls."

"Dancing girls!" exclaimed the treasurer, surprised.

"Yes, dancing girls", replied the sage gravely. "I only need a few, but they must be young and beautiful, so that I may enjoy contemplating their youth and beauty".

Whilst Ibrahim the philosopher spent his days studying in his palatial cave, the "peace-loving" Aben Habuz amused himself by carrying out furious campaigns from his tower. For many years he baited his enemies into attacking him, until in the end no one dared invade his territories. Over time, the old monarch began to miss his favourite pastime, becoming bitter with the monotonous quiet of peace.

After some time, one day the magic warrior turned round suddenly and, lowering his lance, pointed towards the Guadix mountains. Aben Habuz went up to his tower but the magic table that was in that direction was quiet and not a single warrior was moving. Surprised, the king sent out a detachment of horsemen to scour the mountains. After three days, the scouts came back and reported:

"We have searched all the mountain passes and all we have found is a young Christian woman who is exceptionally beautiful; we have captured her and brought her back with us."

"Young and exceptionally beautiful!" exclaimed Aben Habuz, his eyes kindling in anticipation. "Bring her to me!"

So the beautiful damsel was presented. She was dressed finely in the style of the Spaniards at the time of the Arab conquest. Her dark flashing eyes were like sparks to a flame for the old Aben Habuz. Her charming waist made him lose all sense and, frantic and beside himself, he asked her:

"Oh, beautiful woman! Who are you? What is your name?"

"I am the daughter of a Christian prince, who was lord and master of his kingdom and is now held captive after his armies were destroyed as if by magic".

"Beware, oh King!" said Ibrahim suddenly. "This damsel may be some evil spirit sent from the north. They often take on a seductive form to trick their unsuspecting victims. I think I can see witchcraft in her eyes and gestures. She must be the enemy the talisman pointed out".

"Son of Abu Ayub", replied the King, "you are undoubtedly very wise and far-sighted, but you are no expert on the ways of women! I see no harm in this damsel: she is truly beautiful and I take great pleasure looking upon her".

"Listen, oh king!" answered the astrologer. "I have brought you many victories through my magic talisman, but I have never shared any of the spoils; give me then this captive, so that I can find solace in my solitude listening to her playing the silver lyre. If she is, as I suspect, a witch, I will provide you with an antidote against her curse."

"What! More women?" cried Aben Habuz. "Don't you have enough dancers to keep you amused?"

"Yes, I have quite a few dancing girls, it is true, but I have no woman to sing to me. It would give me great solace to have music to refresh my mind when it is weary through study".

"You and your requests be damned!" exclaimed the king. "This damsel is mine and I shall keep her!"

The sage withdrew to his cave, not before repeatedly trying to warn the king about his dangerous prisoner.

But the king did not listen to his advice and gave free reign to his passion. He turned the Zacatin markets high and low buying the most precious products from the Orient: silks, precious stones, trinkets, exquisite perfumes and anything imaginable for his beautiful captive.

But in spite of all the splendours the old lover plied her with, he could never claim to have won over the princess's heart. Although she never frowned on him, she did not smile on him either, and when he declared his amorous passion for her, she responded by playing her silver lyre. There must have been some kind of magic in the chords coming from that lyre, as it immediately had a dramatic effect on the old man, causing him to fall into a deep sleep.

While the royal lover spent his days in a state of stupor and infatuation, rumours and grumbling among the people of Granada grew and grew due to the squandering caused by his favourite's lethal songs. Meanwhile, the dangers intensified and the famous talisman proved ineffective in dealing with them. The insurgents reached as far as Aben Habuz's palace. But suddenly the subdued warrior spirit of the king came back to life, and he quashed the insurrection.

When quiet was restored again, Aben Habuz sought out the astrologer. He approached him with a conciliatory tone and said:

"Oh, wise son of Abu Ayub! You did well to warn me of the dangers of the beautiful captive. Tell me, you who avoids danger so easily, what should I do to in order to be safe in the future?"

"Leave that young infidel immediately, as she is the cause of everything".

"I would rather abandon my kingdom!" retorted Aben Habuz firmly.

"You are at risk of losing both", replied Ibrahim.

"Don't be so harsh and mistrustful, oh profound philosopher! Consider the double affliction of a monarch and a lover, and find some way to free me from the disaster which threatens me".

The astrologer looked at him for a moment, frowning.

"And what would you give me if I provide the retreat you wish for?"

"You can choose your reward".

"Oh king, have you heard of the garden of Irem, the jewel of Arabia Felix?"

"I have heard of this garden, which is mentioned in the Koran. I have also heard pilgrims coming from the Mecca talking about its wonders, but I had thought they were just fables, as are many stories told by travellers who have visited faraway countries".

"Aben Habuz, everything they say about the palace and the garden of Irem is true. I have seen it with my own eyes. A palace and garden like that could be built here, on the mountain that looks over the city. Do I not know all the secrets of magic?"

"Oh, wise son of Abu Ayub!" cried Aben Habuz, frantic with anxiety. "You are a great traveller who has seen and studied wondrous things! Make me a palace like that one and ask for what you will of me, even if it be half of my kingdom".

"Bah!" replied the astrologer, "you know I am an old philosopher who is happy with very little. The only thing I ask for is that you give me the first beast, and the load it is carrying, that enters through the magic gates of the garden".

The monarch gladly agreed to such a modest demand and the astrologer began his work. Upon the top of the hill, above his underground cave, he had a great portal and barbican built, in the centre of an impregnable tower.

An outer hall or vestibule led on to the portal, guarded with solid doors. On the keystone of the portal, the astrologer carved a large key; on the outer keystone of the arch of the hall, higher than that of the portal, he engraved a gigantic hand. These symbols were powerful talismans to which he muttered some words in an unknown language.

Once the work was finished, he shut himself up for two days in his astrological hall, muttering secret incantations. The next day, as night was falling, he appeared before Aben Habuz and said:

"I have finally finished my work, oh King! On top of the hill is the most exquisite palace the human mind could ever conceive of; no man's heart could desire more. The whole mountain has become a paradise of delightful gardens, cool fountains and perfumed baths. Like the garden of Irem, it is protected by powerful spells which hide it from mortals, except for those who possess the secret of its talisman.

"Enough!" exclaimed Aben Habuz joyfully. "Tomorrow at dawn we will go and take possession of it."

At first light the next day, Aben Habuz set out on his way, accompanied by some of his faithful servants, climbing up the narrow path of the hill on horseback. At his side, mounted on a white palfrey, was the Christian princess, splendid in all her finery. The astrologer went up on foot, as he never rode.

The king wanted to look at the towers of the palace and the vaulted terraces of the gardens, but he could not see anything.

"That is the mystery and the safeguard of the palace", the astrologer told him. "Nothing can be distinguished until you pass the threshold of the enchanted hall and go inside".

When they reached the barbican, the astrologer stopped and showed the King the magic hand and the key that were carved into the portal and the arch.

"These are the amulets which guard the entrance to this paradise", he said. "Until the hand comes down and picks up the key, no mortal power or magic trick shall be able to bring harm to the lord of these mountains".

While Aben Habuz was caught up in admiring all that he saw, the princess's palfrey went forward a few steps and entered the hall, reaching the centre of the barbican.

"Behold", cried the astrologer, "the reward you promised me: the first beast, and the load it carries, to enter through the magic door".

"Son of Abu Ayub!" the King replied angrily. "What kind of trick is this? You know very well the meaning of my promise: the first beast with its load to enter the portal. Take the strongest mule from my stables, load it with the most precious objects from my treasury and it is yours. But do not try and take the princess, the joy of my heart".

"What would I do with such riches?" replied the astrologer disdainfully. "Do I not have the *Book of Wisdom* by the wise Solomon, through which I can possess the secret treasures of the earth? The princess belongs to me by right; the royal word is pledged and I claim the damsel as my own".

"Vile son of the desert! You may be wise in all of the arts, but you must recognise me as your lord. Do not try and play with your king".

"My lord...! My lord...!" said the astrologer sarcastically, "the monarch of a little mound of earth who thinks he can dictate to the one who possesses the secrets of magic! Have fun, Aben Habuz. Reign over your little kingdom and enjoy that crazy paradise, while I meanwhile will laugh at your expense in my philosophical retirement".

Saying this, he seized the bridle of the palfrey and, beating the earth with his staff, sank into the centre of the barbican along with the beautiful princess. The earth then closed over them, without leaving any trace of the opening through which they had disappeared.

Aben Habuz, struck dumb at first, soon came to his senses and ordered a thousand workers to dig the site. But the more they tried to dig, the more useless it was: the mountain resisted all their efforts, and when they managed to dig a little deeper, the earth closed over the hole again.

From then on, the top of the mountain, where the palace and garden had once been, turned into wasteland, and the promised paradise remained hidden forever.

To add to his misfortunes, Aben Habuz's enemies, knowing that he was no longer protected by any magical influence, began to invade his land. And so the unfortunate king spent the rest of his life tormented by disturbances and troubles.

Aben Habuz died and was buried several centuries ago. The Alhambra was built afterwards on this famous hill, and in many ways resembled the marvels of the garden of Irem. The enchanted barbican still exists, protected no doubt by the magic hand and the key, which currently form the Gate of Justice, the main entrance to the fortress. Underneath this gate the old astrologer still remains in his underground hall, dozing on his divan, lulled to sleep by the chords of the enchanted princess's silver lyre.

On summer nights the sentinels who guard this gate often hear the sound of music, and doze off at their posts under its powerful influence. Sleep is so irresistible there that even those who keep watch during the day are often found nodding off on benches. All of this, according to ancient legends, will continue to happen: the princess will remain a prisoner under the astrologer's power, and he will stay in a magical slumber until the day of the final judgement, unless the hand grasps the key and undoes the whole spell of this enchanted hill.

# Pilgrim of Love

**HERE WAS ONCE** a sultan of Granada who had only one son, called Ahmed. The astrologers made many favourable predictions about him, saying that he would be a blessed prince and fortunate sovereign. They did however warn that "he would easily fall in love and could be in grave danger due to a passion he would not be able to resist. If he could be stopped from falling in love until he was of mature age, then all these risks could be kept at bay."

To prevent these foretold dangers, the king decided to keep the prince locked up where he would never be able to see the face of any woman, or ever hear about the word love. For this purpose he had a beautiful palace called the Generalife built, on the hill that looked over the Alhambra. It was surrounded by lush gardens, but enclosed by high walls.

The monarch shut up the young prince in this palace, entrusting him to the care and instruction of Bonabben, a wise, severe philosopher who had spent most of his life in Egypt studying hieroglyphics and observing tombs and pyramids.

"Take all the necessary precautions so that my will is done", the king said to him. "Bear in mind that if my son finds out anything about love, it will cost you your head".

"Your Majesty may rest assured about what happens to your son, as I am by my head", responded the prince's new tutor.

So he grew up under the watchful eye of the philosopher, locked up within the palace and its gardens. He listened patiently to his long, complicated lessons, which turned the young prince into an amazingly knowledgeable young man, but he grew up in complete ignorance about what love was.

Time went by and the prince enjoyed walking through the gardens and meditating by the fountains. He developed a taste for music and poetry, both so closely related to love. It was to be expected therefore that the philosopher Bonabben became alarmed and tried to counteract these pastimes by giving him an intense course of algebra, a science which the prince did not seem to like.

"I cannot bear it!"

From then on he watched his pupil anxiously, and saw that the innate tenderness of his nature was developing. Ahmed wandered through the Generalife gardens with heightened feelings, not knowing the cause of them. At times he would sit and drift into delectable daydreams, or else he would strum extremely sentimental tunes on his lute, which he would then toss aside with venom. He would then sigh and burst into strange cries.

Bonabben was alarmed at his pupil's state of agitation. So he quickly removed him from the charms of the garden and shut him up in the highest tower in the Generalife.

So that the prince did not get bored, Bonabben instructed him in the language of birds. The young prince's eyes brightened and he studied them so avidly that soon he was as knowledgeable about them as his master.

Thanks to this, Ahmed became friends with an owl, a very wise-looking bird. The owl's main interest was metaphysics, and the prince found his lectures on this unbearable.

After chatting to a bat who had very limited knowledge about anything, he discovered a very talkative, but very nervous swallow. The swallow rarely stayed quiet long enough for the prince to be able to have a conversation with him.

Winter passed and spring came round again with its lush bloom, bringing with it the happy time when birds make their nests. Suddenly a sweet melody could be heard in the woods and gardens of the Generalife. Everywhere the same universal theme could be heard: "Love! Love! Love!" was chanted and responded to in a thousand poetic ways.

The prince listened perplexed in silence, and then said thoughtfully:

"What is this love of which I know not a word?"

As luck would have it, his guardian happened to enter the tower at that moment. The prince went up to greet him anxiously and said to him:

"Oh, Bonabben! You have taught me most of the wisdom of the earth, but there is one thing about which I am in complete ignorance and I would like you to explain to me. Tell me, most profound sage, what is this thing they call love?"

Bonabben trembled and turned pale.

"What could have suggested such a question to you, my dear prince? Where have you learnt such a foolish word?"

The prince led him to the window of the tower.

"Listen, master", he said. The sage listened. A melodic hymn coming from the trees was singing: 'Love!, Love!, Love!'

"Noble prince, close your ears to these seductive chants! Know that love is the cause of half of the woes that inflict wretched mankind. May Allah keep you, dear prince, in complete ignorance of this passion called love!"

"He's lying", thought the prince as he listened to the tuneful chirping of the birds, "there is no sadness in those notes. There is nothing but tenderness and rejoicing. If love is the cause of such affliction, why are these birds not living in dejected solitude?"

But wisely he did not say anything.

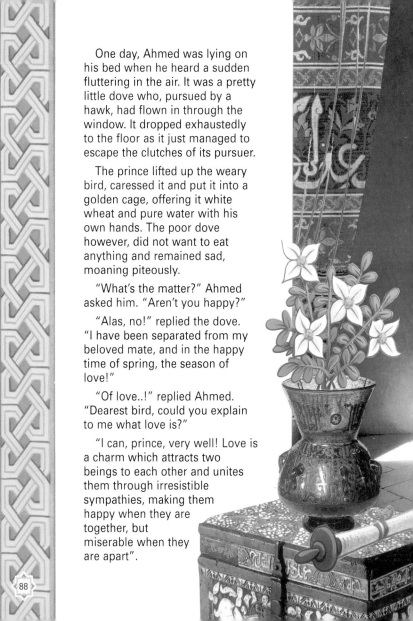

One day, Ahmed was lying on his bed when he heard a sudden fluttering in the air. It was a pretty little dove who, pursued by a hawk, had flown in through the window. It dropped exhaustedly to the floor as it just managed to escape the clutches of its pursuer.

The prince lifted up the weary bird, caressed it and put it into a golden cage, offering it white wheat and pure water with his own hands. The poor dove however, did not want to eat anything and remained sad, moaning piteously.

"What's the matter?" Ahmed asked him. "Aren't you happy?"

"Alas, no!" replied the dove. "I have been separated from my beloved mate, and in the happy time of spring, the season of love!"

"Of love..!" replied Ahmed. "Dearest bird, could you explain to me what love is?"

"I can, prince, very well! Love is a charm which attracts two beings to each other and unites them through irresistible sympathies, making them happy when they are together, but miserable when they are apart".

"Look around you and see how in this wonderful season, all of nature breathes love. Have you wasted all the precious days of your youth without knowing anything about what love is?"

"Now I begin to understand", sighed the prince. "I have felt this restlessness, but did not know the cause of it. But... if love is such a delight and when it goes wrong it is so bitter, let Allah not allow me to disturb the joy of those who love each other!"

And, opening the cage, he took out the dove and carried it to the window, saying:

"Fly, enamoured bird, and rejoice in your loved one!"

The dove fluttered its wings in rapture, flew round in a circle and then swooped off towards the flowery groves of the Darro river.

The prince was left buried deep in bitter thoughts.

When he saw the philosopher Bonabben, his eyes flashed.

"Why have you kept me in this repugnant ignorance?" he said. "Why have you hidden the great mystery and principle of life from me?"

Wise Bonabben had no choice but to reveal to him the astrologers' predictions and the precautions that had been taken with his upbringing in order to avoid the foretold misfortune.

"And now", he added, "my life is in your hands. As soon as your unforgiving father discovers you have in the end learnt what love is, he'll cut my head off".

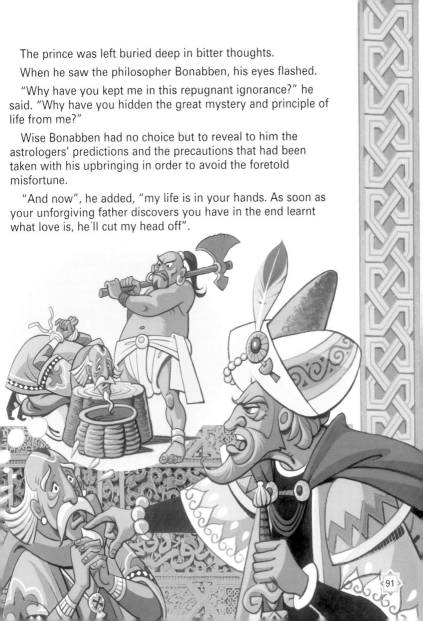

The prince managed to bury what he had learnt at the bottom of his chest, rather than putting the philosopher's life in danger. Perhaps as a reward for his goodness, a few days later Ahmed saw the dove he had freed flying around. The dove came and perched trustingly on Ahmed's shoulder.

"Blessed bird, where have you been since the last time we saw each other?" asked the prince.

"In a faraway land, dear prince, from where I bring happy tidings. Whilst I was flying around, I came upon a wondrous garden. I rested in a tree for a while and saw a radiant princess in the flower of her youth and beauty. She whiled away her days hidden in that retreat, as the garden was surrounded by high walls which allowed no man to enter. And so I thought to myself, 'here is the being created by Heaven to inspire my prince with love".

The dove's tale was a spark to a flame for the heart of the gloomy prince. It was as if all the love latent in his soul until then had suddenly come to the surface to find its missing object. He fell deeply in love with the princess and immediately decided to write her a letter declaring his most ardent love and complaining of the ill-fated imprisonment which prevented him from going to look for her.

He added tender poetry written with moving eloquence, as he was already a natural poet and was all the more so since he was inspired by love. The prince addressed his letter:

*To the unknown beauty
From the captive prince Ahmed*

Away, trusty messenger", he ordered the dove. "Do not rest until you have delivered this missive to she who possesses my heart".

The dove soared away.

Day after day the prince waited for him to come back, but in vain. At last, one evening as the sun was setting, the faithful bird suddenly fluttered into his room and then expired at his feet. A hunter's arrow had pierced through his heart and killed him.

The prince knelt down, grief-stricken, and noticed that the dove had a string of pearls round its neck, with a small enamelled picture attached to it. It was a portrait of a beautiful princess in the flower of her youth.

The prince gazed at the beautiful portrait in rapture, until his eyes brimmed with tears. Finally Ahmed came to a decision. "I will flee from this palace, which is like a prison to me", he said, "and I will travel the whole world in search of this princess".

But how could he manage to escape at night, when he did not know the country? Then Ahmed remembered the owl; as the owl usually flew at night, he should know all the short cuts and best night-time routes. So he went to look for him.

"Do not be offended, oh worthy owl," the prince implored. "Stop meditating with the stars for a while and help me to escape. One day I will be sultan, and then I shall award you with a position of honour".

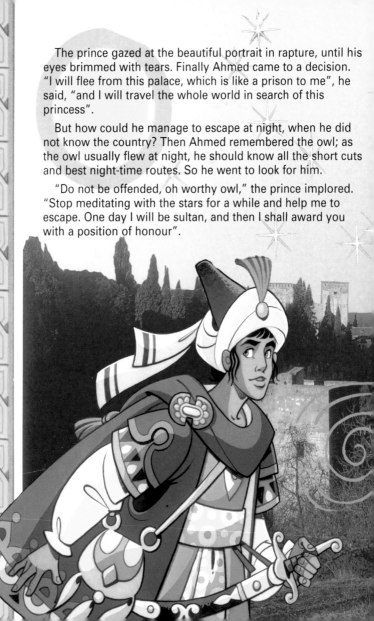

The owl, although he was a philosopher who was above the ordinary needs of life, was not without ambition. So in the end he agreed to flee with the prince, guiding him in his pilgrimage and mentoring him.

The prince escaped that same night from the Generalife, guided by the owl. The owl advised him to go on to Cordoba and look for the great Abderramán palm tree, which stood in the courtyard of the main mosque. There they would find a great voyager who could guide them further.

When they arrived in Cordoba, they found who they were looking for - a famous parrot who had visited many foreign courts.

The prince spoke:

"Tell me, incomparable parrot, in the course of your travels have you ever come across the original of this portrait?"

The parrot grasped the miniature with one of its claws, turned his head from side to side and examined it carefully, eventually crying out:

"Of course I have! This is the unforgettable princess Aldegunda.

"Princess Aldegunda!" echoed the prince. "And where can I find her?"

"You must go to Toledo. She is the only daughter of the Christian king of Toledo and she is shut up from the world until her seventeenth birthday, because of some predictions made by astrologers", the parrot told him.

"That sounds familiar... It must be fate. God wants us to be together. Listen to me, my dear parrot: I am heir to a kingdom and one day I shall sit on a throne. Help me to reach this princess and I shall make you a councillor in my kingdom".

"With all my heart," replied the parrot. "But let it be, if possible, only an honorary title, as us sages detest hard work".

The three travellers left Cordoba and crossed the arid passes of the Morena mountains and the stifling plains of La Mancha and Castile. Finally they made out a fortified city whose walls were built on a rocky escarpment, with the Tagus river swirling around its feet. They had reached Toledo.

"Observe, oh prince!" said the parrot. "This is the abode of your long-sought princess".

The prince directed his gaze towards where the parrot was pointing and saw a sumptuous palace by the banks of the river.

He stared at it in wonder, his heart beating fast.

Looking at it more closely, he noticed that the garden walls were very high, making them impossible to climb. Several patrols of armed guards were walking around outside.

The prince turned to the parrot and said:

"Oh, clever being who knows how to talk like men, go to the garden and look for my beloved. Tell her that Prince Ahmed, a pilgrim of love guided by the stars, has arrived!"

The parrot, proud of his embassy, flew to the garden and perched on the balcony of a pavilion that was on the edge of the river. There he discovered the princess reclining on a cushion with her eyes staring at a piece of paper. Tear after tear rolled gently down her cheeks.

The parrot said to her with a gallant air:

"Wipe away your years, oh most beautiful of all princesses! I have come to cheer your heart. I have come to announce that Ahmed, Prince of Granada, has arrived in your quest.

Hearing these words, the princess's eyes sparkled more than the diamonds in her crown.

"Oh parrot! What happy tidings you bring, for I was down at heart and deadly ill. Fly and tell him that the passionate sentences in his letter are engraved on my heart, and his poetry has fed my soul. Tell him also to prepare to demonstrate his love with the force of arms, as tomorrow is my seventeenth birthday. A big tournament will be held in my honour, in which several princes will fight, and my hand will be given as a prize to the victor".

The parrot soared off into the sky and, crossing over the poplar groves, arrived back where the prince was waiting for him. Ahmed's joy heartened his soul. However, he went pale when he heard about the tournament, as he had never fought before. Then the owl broke his silence.

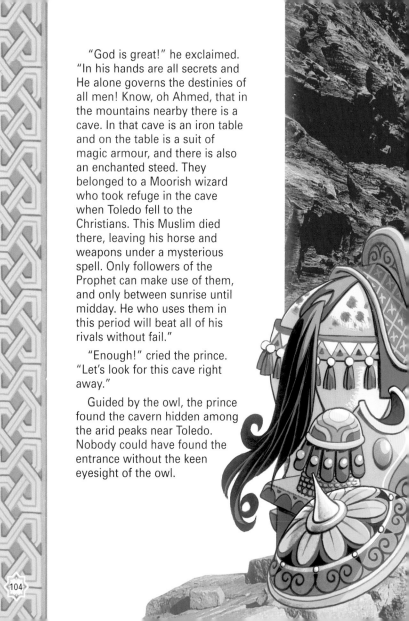

"God is great!" he exclaimed. "In his hands are all secrets and He alone governs the destinies of all men! Know, oh Ahmed, that in the mountains nearby there is a cave. In that cave is an iron table and on the table is a suit of magic armour, and there is also an enchanted steed. They belonged to a Moorish wizard who took refuge in the cave when Toledo fell to the Christians. This Muslim died there, leaving his horse and weapons under a mysterious spell. Only followers of the Prophet can make use of them, and only between sunrise until midday. He who uses them in this period will beat all of his rivals without fail."

"Enough!" cried the prince. "Let's look for this cave right away."

Guided by the owl, the prince found the cavern hidden among the arid peaks near Toledo. Nobody could have found the entrance without the keen eyesight of the owl.

Indeed, inside the cave was the iron table, with a set of magic armour and a lance resting upon it. Close by was an Arabian steed saddled and ready for battle.

The day of the tournament finally dawned. The fairest ladies in the kingdom, commoners and courtiers, had gathered for the event. There was a general murmur of surprise when Princess Aldegunda appeared. Her beauty eclipsed that of all of the other ladies present and inflamed all the more the princes who were aspiring for her hand, keen to enter into battle. The princess, however, looked melancholy; her cheeks changed colour constantly and her eyes flitted incessantly and anxiously towards the group of knights dressed and ready for combat. The bugles were about to ring, signalling the start of combat, when the herald announced the arrival of another gentleman – it was Ahmed.

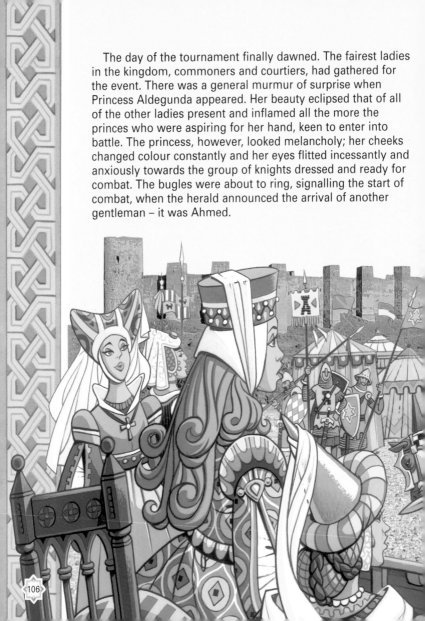

The prince's dashing figure astonished everyone, even more so when he was announced as "the pilgrim of love". His opponents surrounded him with a threatening and arrogant demeanour, one of them even daring to mock the prince's dark skin and his "pilgrim of love" alias.

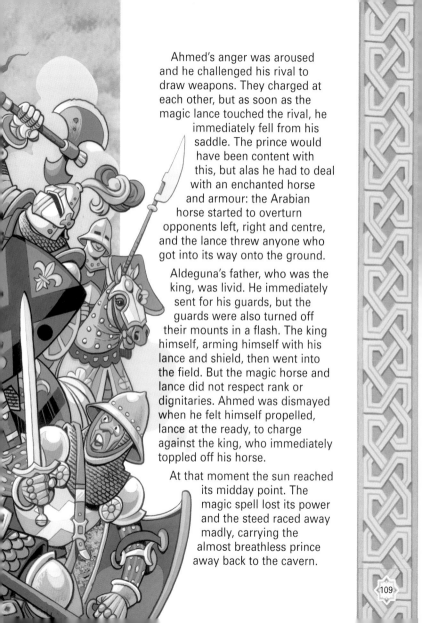

Ahmed's anger was aroused and he challenged his rival to draw weapons. They charged at each other, but as soon as the magic lance touched the rival, he immediately fell from his saddle. The prince would have been content with this, but alas he had to deal with an enchanted horse and armour: the Arabian horse started to overturn opponents left, right and centre, and the lance threw anyone who got into its way onto the ground.

Aldeguna's father, who was the king, was livid. He immediately sent for his guards, but the guards were also turned off their mounts in a flash. The king himself, arming himself with his lance and shield, then went into the field. But the magic horse and lance did not respect rank or dignitaries. Ahmed was dismayed when he felt himself propelled, lance at the ready, to charge against the king, who immediately toppled off his horse.

At that moment the sun reached its midday point. The magic spell lost its power and the steed raced away madly, carrying the almost breathless prince away back to the cavern.

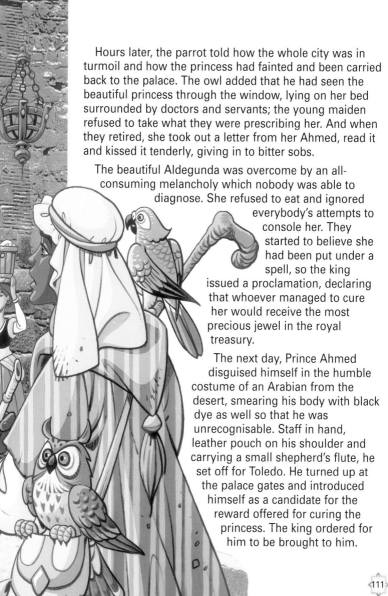

Hours later, the parrot told how the whole city was in turmoil and how the princess had fainted and been carried back to the palace. The owl added that he had seen the beautiful princess through the window, lying on her bed surrounded by doctors and servants; the young maiden refused to take what they were prescribing her. And when they retired, she took out a letter from her Ahmed, read it and kissed it tenderly, giving in to bitter sobs.

The beautiful Aldegunda was overcome by an all-consuming melancholy which nobody was able to diagnose. She refused to eat and ignored everybody's attempts to console her. They started to believe she had been put under a spell, so the king issued a proclamation, declaring that whoever managed to cure her would receive the most precious jewel in the royal treasury.

The next day, Prince Ahmed disguised himself in the humble costume of an Arabian from the desert, smearing his body with black dye as well so that he was unrecognisable. Staff in hand, leather pouch on his shoulder and carrying a small shepherd's flute, he set off for Toledo. He turned up at the palace gates and introduced himself as a candidate for the reward offered for curing the princess. The king ordered for him to be brought to him.

"Oh most powerful king!" said Ahmed. "Before you stands a Bedouin Arab who has spent most of his life in the lonely desert, which is the haunt of evil spirits that torment poor shepherds. To counteract this evilness we discovered an antidote – music. The tunes we play and sing expel these evil spirits."

The king, full of hope, led him to the high tower where his daughter's chamber was. Through the half-open windows, the princess could be seen lying prostrate on the bed.

First, Ahmed played some Arabian melodies on his pastoral pipe.

The princess remained indifferent, until the prince put his pipe aside and sang the amorous verses of the letter in which he had declared his passion.

The princess recognised the words and was suddenly overcome with joy. She lifted her head and listened, whilst her eyes brimmed with tears which then ran down her cheeks. Her breast heaved softly with emotion.

The king, guessing his daughter's wishes, commanded Ahmed to be brought in front of the princess.

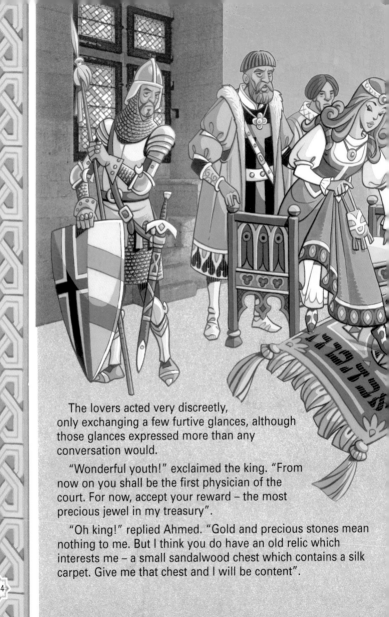

The lovers acted very discreetly,
only exchanging a few furtive glances, although
those glances expressed more than any
conversation would.

"Wonderful youth!" exclaimed the king. "From
now on you shall be the first physician of the
court. For now, accept your reward – the most
precious jewel in my treasury".

"Oh king!" replied Ahmed. "Gold and precious stones mean
nothing to me. But I think you do have an old relic which
interests me – a small sandalwood chest which contains a silk
carpet. Give me that chest and I will be content".

They brought the sandalwood chest and took out the rug, woven from green silk and covered with Hebrew characters and strange symbols.

"This carpet used to cover the throne of the wise Solomon, and is therefore worthy of being placed at the feet of beauty", said the prince.

So saying, he spread it beneath an ottoman that had been brought for the princess. Then he sat down at her feet.

"Who shall oppose what is written in the book of fate?" he cried. "Know, oh king, that your daughter and I have loved each other in secret for a long time. See, therefore, that it is I, the pilgrim of love!"

And at that moment the carpet rose into the air, carrying off the prince and princess with it. The king was incensed, and gathered a powerful army. They set off to Granada in pursuit of the fugitives, sending on a herald to ask for his daughter to be returned.

The sultan of Granada came out in person with all his court in attendance to meet him, and in him they recognised the Arabian minstrel. Ahmed had taken the throne of Granada after his father had died, and had made the beautiful Aldegunda his sultana.

The Christian king was easily pacified when he found out that his daughter continued true to her faith. And so, instead of bloody battles, there were many festivities and much rejoicing. After this, the king returned to Toledo, extremely content.

And the young couple continued to reign happily and wisely from the Alhambra.

# The Moor's Legacy

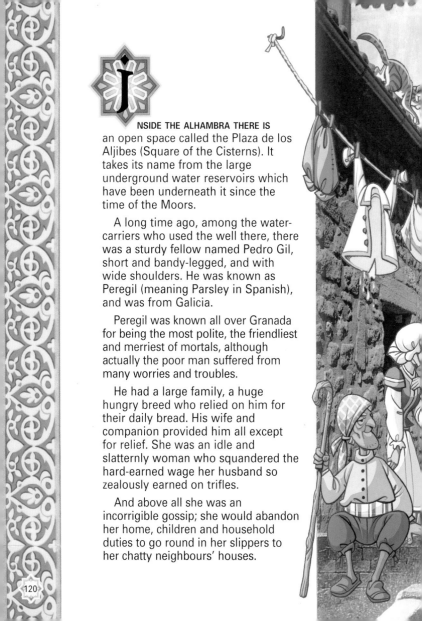

**I**NSIDE THE ALHAMBRA THERE IS an open space called the Plaza de los Aljibes (Square of the Cisterns). It takes its name from the large underground water reservoirs which have been underneath it since the time of the Moors.

A long time ago, among the water-carriers who used the well there, there was a sturdy fellow named Pedro Gil, short and bandy-legged, and with wide shoulders. He was known as Peregil (meaning Parsley in Spanish), and was from Galicia.

Peregil was known all over Granada for being the most polite, the friendliest and merriest of mortals, although actually the poor man suffered from many worries and troubles.

He had a large family, a huge hungry breed who relied on him for their daily bread. His wife and companion provided him all except for relief. She was an idle and slatternly woman who squandered the hard-earned wage her husband so zealously earned on trifles.

And above all she was an incorrigible gossip; she would abandon her home, children and household duties to go round in her slippers to her chatty neighbours' houses.

It was late one summer night, and all the watercarriers had stopped working for the evening.

ally hot day and there were
irsty for water. So Peregil, as a
er, said to himself as he
will make one more trip to the
tle ones' stew on Sunday".
the hill towards the

, it was completely deserted
ger dressed like a Moor. The
e stone benches in the
d looked at him with a
fear, but the Moor beckoned

"I am weak and ill", he said. "Help me to return to the
city and I will pay you double what you can earn from the
water".

The poor water carrier's sensitive heart was moved by
the stranger's entreaty and he replied:

"God would not want me to receive any reward for a
basic act of human kindness".

So he helped the Moor to mount his donkey and set off
with him slowly down towards Granada. When they
reached the city, the water carrier asked him where he
needed to go.

"Alas!" said the Moor faintly. "I do not have a house or
a home, as I am a stranger in this land. Let me spend
tonight in your house and I shall reward you splendidly".

Thus good old Peregil found himself unexpectedly
landed with a guest. But he was too compassionate to
deny a night of hospitality to a poor old man who found
himself in such a dreadful situation. So he led the Arab to
his abode.

"Who is this infidel you bring to my house at this late hour? You will have the Inquisition onto us!" his wife screamed at him.

"Calm down, wife!" replied the Galician. "He is a poor, sick stranger, with no friends and no bed for the night. Would you have me throw him out onto the streets for him to perish?"

And so the poor water carrier helped the poorly Muslim to dismount from the donkey and offered him a rush mat and sheepskin in the coolest part of the house, which was the only bed the poverty-stricken man could offer.

Shortly afterwards the Moor was overcome by convulsions which were beyond the medical skills of the simple water carrier. The Moor called Peregil to his side during one of his breaks from the convulsions and said to him in a low voice:

"I know my end is near. If I die, I leave you this box as a reward for your charity. And so saying, he opened his cloak to reveal a little sandalwood box that was strapped to his body.

"May God let you live many years, my friend, to enjoy your treasure – whatever it may be", the kindly Galician replied.

The Moor shook his head, put his hand on the box and went to say something about it, but his convulsions returned more violently than ever, and after a while he took his last breath. The water carrier's wife was furious.

"This has happened because of your silly nonsense", she said. "You always get yourself into these scrapes by helping others out. What will become of us when they find this body in our house?"

Poor Peregil was also in anguish, until after a time he had a clever idea.

"It's not daytime yet", he said. "I can take the corpse out of the city and bury it in the sandbanks of the Genil river. No one saw the Moor come into our house and no one need know of his death".

So said, and it was done. His wife helped him to wrap the old man's body in the mat on which he had died. Then they put this across the donkey's back and the man set off towards the river.

But as bad luck would have it, a barber called Pedrillo Pedrugo lived opposite the water carrier – he was the biggest gossip in the world, always prying into other people's lives and causing trouble.

The busybody barber heard Peregil arrive at a suspiciously late hour of the night and then listened to the remonstrations of the water carrier's wife and children. He immediately leant out of the little window he used to spy on the outside world and saw his neighbour enter the house with a man dressed like a Moor. This was so strange an occurrence that Pedrillo Pedrugo could not sleep a wink all night. Every five minutes he would put his head to the little window and watch the light that shone through the chinks of his neighbour's door, until at length he saw him go out before daybreak with a very heavily laden donkey.

Pedrillo got dressed in the blink of an eye and followed the water carrier at a distance. He then saw him dig a hole in the sandy bank of the Genil, and bury a large object which appeared to be a body.

The barber hurried back home, tucked his barber's basin under his arm and went to the mayor's house, a daily customer of his.

The mayor had just got up when the barber arrived. Pedrillo Pedrugo made him sit in a chair, put a cloth round his neck and filled the basin with hot water whilst he chatted.

"What terrible events! What strange happenings! A robbery, a murder and a burial, all in one night!"

"I beg your pardon! What are you saying?" exclaimed the mayor.

"I'm saying", continued the barber, "that Peregil the Galician has robbed and murdered a Moor and buried him this very night".

"And how do you know all of this?" the mayor asked him.

The barber told him all he had seen.

It so happened that this mayor was the most greedy and insatiable despot in Granada. He presumed the case in question was a robbery and murder, and that the spoils of the robbery must be considerable... With this reasoning, he sent for his most trusted bailiff, a sleuth with a tipstaff in his hand. This bailiff was so diligent that it was no time before he was knocking at Peregil's door. He arrested him and led him with the tipstaff before the judge.

The mayor gave the poor Galician a terrifying look and in a threatening voice that made him fall to his knees shaking, he said:

"Listen, you villain! Do not try and deny your crime because I know everything. You should hang for the crime you have committed, but as I am a compassionate person, I am willing to listen to reason. The man who was killed in your house was a Moor, an infidel who is the enemy of our faith. I am sure you must have killed him in a fit of religious zeal, so I therefore want to be merciful with you. Hand over what you stole from him and we will cover up the whole thing".

The unfortunate water carrier related the whole story of the dying Moor, telling the complete truth, but it was all in vain.

"Are you going to go on pretending that this Moor had no money or jewels, when this was what tempted your greed?" demanded the judge.

"It is as true as I am innocent, sir", replied the water carrier. "He had nothing more on him than a little sandalwood box, which he bequeathed to me as a reward for helping him".

"A sandalwood box! A sandalwood box!" exclaimed the mayor, his pupils lighting up in the hope of there being a precious jewel inside. "Where is this box? Where have you hidden it?"

"Please, your Grace, it is in one of the panniers on my donkey and entirely at the service of your worship", answered Peregil.

No sooner had he pronounced these words when the eager bailiff shot off and came back in a flash with the mysterious sandalwood box. The mayor opened it and everyone came forward to see what treasures lay contained inside... But what a disappointment! There was nothing inside other than a parchment scroll with Arabic characters written on it.

When the mayor recovered from the disappointment and saw that there was no booty to get hold of, he listened dispassionately to Peregil's explanations, which were also corroborated by his wife. Convinced as a result of his innocence, he left him free to go and allowed him to take the sandalwood box and its contents. He did, however, keep the donkey in payment of costs.

Was ever a mortal so punished as poor Peregil for having done a good deed? The unfortunate water carrier was physically and morally injured. He did still manage to endure the cruel sarcasm of his wife however. One night though, he lost his calm. His eyes focused on the sandalwood box, he picked it up and threw it at the floor in a fury, exclaiming:

"I curse the day I laid eyes on you for the first time!" But then, as the box hit the floor, the lid opened completely and the parchment scroll rolled out.

Peregil stood looking at the mysterious scroll in silence, gathering his thoughts. He said to himself: "Who knows! Maybe what is written there is something important!"

So he picked up the parchment, tucked it away close to his chest and the next morning, when he went by the shop of a Moor, native of Tangiers, he asked him to translate the contents.

The Moor read the parchment attentively and told him:

"This manuscript is a formula for recovering a hidden treasure that lies under a spell."

"Bah!" cried Peregil. "What do I need that for? I'm not an enchanter, and I don't know anything about hidden treasures".

And as he said this, he threw the water container on his shoulder, left the scroll in the hands of the Moor and went off around the streets as usual.

But that night as he sat down for a while at dusk, close to the well at the Alhambra, he heard a group of men talking about the enchanted riches left buried by the Moors in various parts of the Alhambra. They all believed that there were amazing treasures hidden in the Tower of the Seven Floors.

This made a great impression of honest Peregil's mind. So much so that bright and early the next day, he went by the Moor's shop and told him what had happened.

"You know Arabic. How about if we go to the tower together and try out the effect of the charm? If it doesn't work, we have lost nothing; if it does, we can share the treasure we find between us", said the water carrier.

"Agreed!" replied the Moor. "But these words must be read at midnight."

They both then settled on trying out the magic that very night. So, much later on, they climbed the Alhambra hill and made their way to the solitary tower, which stood there with an imposing presence amongst the trees.

With the aid of a lantern they managed to find the entrance to a vault which was underneath the tower. They went down a staircase cut into the rock, trembling with fear and full of terror. This led to a damp and dark room where there was another staircase leading to a vault even deeper under the ground. They stopped there for a minute to regain their breath, until they heard the faint chimes of midnight from the bells of the watchtower. Then they lit the end of a yellow taper.

The Moor started to read the parchment hurriedly. He had barely finished when a terrifying noise was heard underground. The earth shook and the ground opened, revealing a stone staircase. They went down quaking with fear and saw in the lamplight another vault covered in Arabic inscriptions. In the centre was an enormous chest that was bolted with seven steel bars. In front of the chest there were several urns filled with gold, silver and precious stones.

They delved in up to the elbows in the largest urn, bringing out handfuls of beautiful Moorish coins, bracelets and ornaments from the same metal, as well as some oriental pearl necklaces that they wound between their fingers. A terrifying noise was suddenly heard.

Petrified, they quickly snatched up some of the riches that were lying next to the chest and did not stop until they had climbed all the stairs out of the tower and saw the stars shining again from between the branches of the trees. They shared the booty between them and decided to come back another time to empty the jars of treasure. Then they set off back down the hill towards Granada.

When they were at the foot of the hill, the cautious Moor whispered some advice in the simple water carrier's ear.

"Peregil my friend", he said, "this matter must be kept top secret. If the mayor finds out, we are done for!"

"You are right", answered the water carrier. "That is very wise".

"Peregil my friend", the Moor repeated, "I am sure you can keep a secret, but you have a wife…"

"My wife shall not hear a word about any of this", replied the water carrier determinedly.

"That's good. I have faith in your discretion and promise", said the Moor.

When he got home, Peregil found his wife sobbing in a corner.

"Goodness!" she said as he came in. "Thank God you have come home, after spending the night gallivanting!"

And she cried:

"Poor me! What will become of me? My house is searched and looted by clerks and bailiffs, and my husband doesn't think about bringing home bread for his family any more, but instead spends day and night out and about with those infidel Moors!"

Honest Peregil was so upset by his wife's outburst that he could not contain his tears. His heart felt as heavy as his pocket and he could not keep it in any longer. So he put his hand in his pocket and brought out three or four fine golden coins and slipped them into his saddened wife's skirts. The poor woman's eyes widened in astonishment, as she could not understand where all this gold could have come from. Before she could get over her amazement, the Galician took out a gold chain and gave it to her, a huge grin spreading over his face.

"The Holy Virgin have mercy on us!" said his wife. "What have you done? Tell me what you have done Peregil! For sure, you have robbed someone, or murdered someone!"

What else could the poor man do? He had no choice but to calm his wife down and dispel all the things she was imagining, by telling her about the good luck he had had. Of course, he first made her promise solemnly to keep it absolutely secret, swearing not to breathe a word of it to any living soul.

Peregil's wife kept the secret surprisingly well. But although she was careful outside the house, she made up for it inside by wearing a string of oriental pearls around her neck, Moorish bracelets on her arms and a diamond tiara on her head. And she could not resist standing by the window to see the effect her attire would have on passers-by.

As luck would have it, the meddling barber Pedrillo Pedrugo happened to be sitting there doing nothing in his shop at that moment, and the glitter of the diamonds caught his watchful eye. He was at his peephole in a flash and recognised the water carrier's shabby wife decked out in all the splendour of a newly-wed Eastern bride. He immediately shot off to the mayor's house and, before the day was over, the unlucky Peregil was dragged before the authorities again.

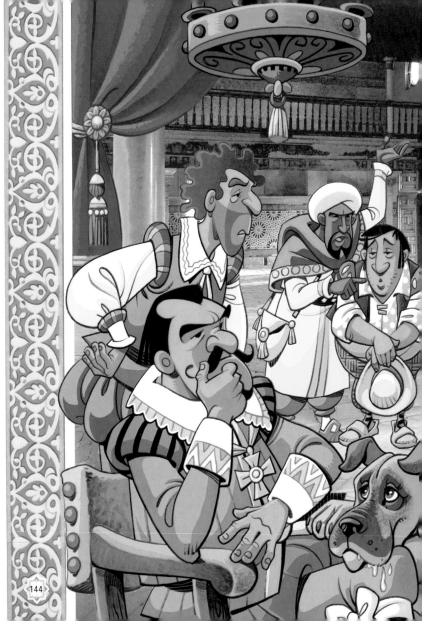

"What is this, you despicable man?" shouted the mayor, furious. "You villain! You shall go to the gallows!"

The terrified water carrier fell on his knees and confessed everything about the incredible way he had gained his riches. The mayor, bailiff and tell-tale barber listened greedily to the fantastic tale of the enchanted treasure. The bailiff was despatched immediately to fetch the Moor who had helped with the magic spell. The Muslim arrived and was frightened out of his wits to find himself in the hands of the law. When he saw the water carrier standing there looking abashed and apprehensive, he understood everything.

"Miserable animal!" he said as he passed him. "Didn't I warn you not to say anything to your wife?"

The Moor's description of events coincided perfectly with his friend's, but the mayor pretended not to believe anything and began to threaten them with prison and a thorough investigation.

"Hold it there, mayor sir!" said the Muslim, recovering his calm and composure. "Do not waste the favours that fortune has brought us by ruining it all. Nobody apart from us knows anything about this affair; let us all keep it a secret between us. There is still a whole treasure trove down there underneath the tower, enough to make us all rich."

The mayor consulted with the bailiff to one side and then said:

"This is a strange story that may be true, but I want to see it for myself. Tonight, therefore, you will repeat the spell in my presence; if the treasure really exists, we will share it amicably between us and not say another word about it. But if this is a trick, do not expect any mercy from me. In the meantime, you shall remain in custody".

The Moor and the water carrier gladly agreed to these terms, convinced that the results would prove their words were true.

Around midnight the mayor, accompanied by the bailiff and the barber, crept out stealthily, all well-armed.

They led the Moor and water carrier as prisoners, taking along the water carrier's sturdy donkey with them to transport all the coveted treasure. They reached the tower without anyone spotting them, tied the donkey up to a fig tree and went down the four floors beneath the tower.

They took out the parchment and the Moor read the form of enchantment. The earth shook as it had before, and the ground opened with a thundering noise, revealing the narrow flight of stairs. The mayor, bailiff and barber were terrified and were not brave enough to go down; the Moor and the water carrier entered the lowest vault however. They took the two largest jars, crammed with golden coins and precious stones, and Peregil carried them up the stairs, saying that this was a much as the donkey could bear.

"We have plenty for now", said the Moor. "We have all the treasure here we can carry without being seen, and enough to become as powerful as we could ever wish for".

"But is there still more treasure left?" asked the mayor.

"The most valuable items are left", said the Moor. "There is a huge coffer filled with pearls and precious stones".

"Well, let's bring that coffer up immediately", shouted the greedy mayor.

"I'm not going down there again", said the Moor stubbornly. "This is enough for any reasonable person; anything more seems unnecessary".

"And I will not bring anymore to load onto my poor donkey and break his back", added the water carrier.

Seeing that their commands, threats and entreaties went unheeded, the mayor turned round to his two companions and said:

"Help me to carry up the coffer and we will share all the contents of it."

No sooner did the Moor see them descend than the ground closed behind them with the terrifying noise. The three proud men remained buried underneath.

"Allah's will has been carried out!" said the Moor devoutly.

There was nothing to be done. So the Moor and the water carrier returned to the city, leading the donkey laden with all the riches. The two lucky partners divided up the loot amicably and fairly.

Both went off after a while to enjoy their wealth in peace in faraway lands. The Moor went back to Tangiers, his native land, and the Galician left for Portugal with his wife, children and donkey. There, Peregil became an important figure, dropping his nickname of Peregil and taking the more impressive title of Don Pedro Gil.

As for the mayor and his cohorts, they remained buried underneath the great Tower of the Seven Floors and are still there bound by the spell today.

# The Page and the Falcon

**MANY YEARS AFTER**

...oors surrendered Granada,
...e city was a frequent favourite
residence for Spanish sovereigns.
But then they were chased away
by the continual earthquakes
which devastated many of the
buildings and shook the old
Moorish towers to their very
foundations.

After a long time, it was
honoured once again, as in days
gone by, by the visit of some
royal personages. The Alhambra,
jewel of the city, had to be
decorated and furnished in a great
hurry to be fit to receive the first
Bourbon king on the Spanish
throne, Philip V, and his wife
Elizabeth, Princess of Parma,
whom he had taken as his second
wife. With the arrival of the court,
the palace's recent deserted aspect
was transformed completely.

Among the persons in the royal
party was a page, a favourite of
the queen, called Ruiz de
Alarcón. He had just turned
eighteen and was slim,
well-turned out and
handsome.

One morning, the boisterous page was wandering around the Generalife woodlands surrounding the Alhambra, taking with him one of the queen's favourite falcons as amusement. Suddenly, the great bird spotted some prey perched in a tree, spread its wings and flew off to pursue it, ignoring the calls of the page. Luckily, the page was able to keep the fugitive bird in sight upon its sudden flight, and eventually he saw it settle on top of the walls of the Princesses Tower.

The page went down into the ravine and approached the tower. There was a small garden in front of it. The youth opened a wicket gate and made his way forward among beds of flowers and thickets of roses until he reached the door of the tower. Although it was closed he was able to peek through a hole and make out the inside of the mysterious bastion.

He saw a beautiful Moorish hall, with exquisitely detailed walls and an alabaster fountain surrounded by flowers. In the centre hung a golden cage with a beautiful little bird inside. Underneath this, on a chair, was a sleeping cat lying among some skeins of silk and other objects of feminine labour. Close to the fountain lay a guitar.

He knocked gently at the door and saw a beautiful face appear briefly from a mullioned window above, and then disappear. The youth waited for the door to be opened, but in vain; there was not the faintest of sounds from within. Had his senses deceived him or was the beautiful apparition perhaps a fairy that inhabited the tower? He knocked again more loudly and, after a little while the same enchanting face appeared a second time, that of a beautiful fifteen-year-old damsel.

The page tipped his plumed hat and asked her, in his most courteous manner, to allow him to go up the tower to pick up his runaway falcon.

"Please forgive me, sir, if I do not open the door", answered the young girl, blushing. "My aunt has forbidden it".

"I beg of you, beautiful girl, this is the queen's favourite falcon. How can I go back to the palace without it?"

"Are you then a gentleman of the court?"

"I am indeed, my charming maid. But I will fall into disgrace with the queen if I lose that falcon".

"Holy Virgin Mary! It is precisely the gentlemen of the court whom my aunt has charged me most insistently never to open the door to!"

"Yes, but she means the wicked gentlemen, and that is all well and good. But I, my dear one, am just a simple and harmless page, who shall be ruined and lost if you deny him this small favour".

The young damsel's heart was touched by the poor page's distress. It would be such a shame for him to ruin his career for so trifling a matter. And surely this young man could not be one of those dangerous courtiers that her aunt had described; on the contrary, how gentle and modest he looked.

The clever page saw that the maiden's defences were beginning to waver, and he redoubled his entreaties in such a moving way that it was not in the damsel's nature to deny him. So, the bashful and tender guardian of the tower came down and opened the door with a trembling hand. If the page had been delighted to glimpse her face through the window, he was even more ecstatic when he was able to view the beautiful Castilian maiden standing right in front of him.

In spite of himself, Ruiz de Alarcón went quickly up the spiral staircase in search of his bird.

He appeared after a short while with the naughty falcon on his hand. The damsel, meanwhile, had sat down next to the fountain in the hall and was winding a skein of silk. In her discomfiture however, she dropped the ball of silk on the floor.

The page sprang forward gallantly to pick it up and, kneeling on the ground, presented it to her. As the young woman stretched her hand out to receive it, the lad planted an ardent kiss upon it.

"Good heavens!" exclaimed the blushing maid, filled with confusion, as she had never received such a kiss.

The humble page made a thousand apologies, reassuring her that it was a court custom to express the deepest of respect in this way.

The young girl's vexation (if she was indeed vexed) abated quickly, but she continued to be agitated and bewildered, as she sat down again blushing more than ever and looking increasingly crestfallen. Although she was focused on her task, she was only managing to tangle the skein of silk she was trying to wind.

The crafty predator was aware of the confusion he had sewn in the young girl's heart, but though he had enjoyed great success amongst the ladies of the court due to his grace and confidence, he found himself feeling intimidated, stammering in the presence of an innocent young girl of fifteen.

161

In short, the simple damsel had more effective guardians in her modesty and innocence than in the locks and bolts that her watchful aunt kept her behind. And yet, what female heart could remain indifferent to the first awakenings of love? The young girl, for all her candour and simplicity, understood instinctively everything that the stuttering tongue of the page could not express, and her heart overflowed with joy to see a lover surrendering at her feet for the first time...

The page's discomfort, although sincere, did not last long. But just as the man was regaining his habitual aplomb and composure, he heard a shrill voice some distance away.

"It's my aunt, coming back from mass!" shouted the damsel, afraid. "Sir, I beg you to leave".

"Not until you give me that rose in your hair to remember you by".

She unwound it hastily from her dark locks and said, blushing and confused:

"Take it, but leave now, please, I beg you".

The page took the flower, covering the beautiful hand that offered it to him with kisses at the same time. He donned his hat and placed the falcon on his fist, then slipped out into the garden, taking with him the beautiful Jacinta's heart.

When the jealous aunt entered the tower, she noticed her niece's agitation and the untidy hall. Jacinta explained it all away in a few words:

"A falcon flew right into the room in pursuit of its prey".

"God save us and come to our aid! So falcons are coming right into the tower? Goodness me! The poor little bird is not even safe in its cage anymore!"

The watchful Fredegunda was a very old and experienced servant. She viewed what she referred to as "the opposite sex" with fear and mistrust.

Her niece, orphan of an officer who had died on the battlefield, had been educated in a convent and had only recently been taken out of that holy place to be placed under the care of her watchful aunt. Under her vigilant wardenship the poor creature lived in seclusion, like a bud that blooms hidden amongst the bushes. Her fresh and virginal beauty had certainly caught people's eyes and been much admired, in spite of her secluded existence. In line with the poetic customs of the Andalusian people, her neighbours gave her the name of "the Rose of the Alhambra".

Meanwhile, King Philip V decided to cut short his stay in Granada and departed suddenly with all his entourage. The suspicious Fredegunda watched the royal retinue with a keen eye. When the last standard disappeared from sight, she returned joyfully to her tower, as she no longer had to maintain all her vigilance and care.

But to her great surprise, she saw a fine Arabian colt pawing the ground at the wicket gate of the garden. Then, to her horror, she saw an elegant young man through the rose bushes, sitting tenderly at her niece's feet. Hearing footsteps, the lad hurriedly said his last "adieu" to his loved one, and jumping nimbly over the tangle of reeds and myrtles, he mounted his horse and was out of sight in a flash.

The smitten Jacinta, deeply affected by her loss, did not think about her aunt's reaction and, throwing herself into her arms, burst into a flood of tears.

"Oh my!" she sighed. "He's gone! He's gone! I will never see him again!"

"What has gone? Who has gone? Who was that young man I saw at your feet?"

"A queen's page, dear aunt, who came to say goodbye to me".

"A queen's page, child!" shouted Fredegunda hysterically. "And when did you meet this queen's page?"

"The day the falcon flew into the tower. It was the queen's falcon and he came after it".

"Oh, innocent child! You must know that there are no falcons as fearsome as those libertine pages, and especially when they pray upon as inexperienced birds as you..."

Days, weeks and months went by, and nothing more was heard of the queen's page. Autumn came with its torrential rain and the page did not come back. Winter passed and spring came round again, with the singing of the birds, and still nobody knew anything more of the page. Meanwhile the unhappy Jacinta became pale and melancholy. She abandoned her occupations and pastimes, her skeins of silk remained unwound, her guitar was silent. She no longer heard the tweeting of the birds and her eyes, formerly sparkling and bright, became dull through so much secret weeping.

One summer night at quite a late hour, the damsel remained in the hall of the tower, sitting next to the alabaster fountain, where the disloyal lover had knelt down and kissed her hand for the first time. The saddened damsel's heart was in shreds and her tears flowed abundantly, falling into the fountain drop by drop. The water slowly started to get agitated and to boil, bubbles forming, until the beautiful figure of a woman clad in Moorish dress appeared in front of her very eyes.

Jacinta was so frightened that she fled at once. The following morning she told her aunt what she had seen, but the good lady believed that it was all the imaginings of her disturbed dreams. She had probably fallen asleep and been dreaming next to the supposedly magical fountain.

"You must have been thinking about the story of the three Moorish princesses who lived in this tower in times gone by", she added, "and that made you dream about them".

"What story is that, aunt?"

"Have you never heard the story of the three princesses Zayda, Zorayda and Zorahayda, who were shut up in this tower by their father the Muslim king? They decided to run away with three Christian gentlemen. Only the first two carried the plan through, as the youngest one lacked the courage to follow them. And that one, Zorahayda, is the one who, according to legend, died in the tower".

"Now I remember having heard this story", said Jacinta, "and I often cried about the poor Zorahayda's misfortunes".

"You are right to feel pain for her misfortunes", continued the aunt, "as Zorahayda's lover was one of your ancestors. He wept for his adored Moorish princess for many years, but eventually time healed his pain and he married a noble Spanish lady, whom you are descended from".

The following night, when all was quiet, her curiosity overcame her fear, and Jacinta went to sit by the fountain again. No sooner had the bell of the distant watchtower chimed midnight, than the fountain stirred again and the water began to boil until the strange vision appeared. She was young and beautiful and her dress was adorned with rich jewels. In her hand she carried a lute. Jacinta trembled but grew calmer when she heard the sweet, dulcet tones of the apparition and saw the affectionate expression on her melancholic, pale face.

"Daughter of mortals!" she said. "What ails you? Why do your tears disturb the water in my fountain? Why do your sighs and moans interrupt the tranquil silence of the night?"

"I am crying about men's ingratitude and complaining about my sad loneliness and abandonment".

"Console yourself, my child! Your troubles may well end. See in me a Moorish princess who, like you, was very unlucky in love. A Christian gentleman, your ancestor, captured my heart and would have taken me to his native land and into his church. I would have converted completely, but I lacked the courage to equal my faith and I hesitated at a crucial moment. And so the evil spirit took hold of me and I remain enchanted in this tower until a Christian soul agrees to break the magic spell. Do you wish to do this?"

"Oh, of course I will!" said the young girl, moved.

"Well, come closer and do not be afraid. Put your hand in the fountain, sprinkle the water on me and baptise me according to the customs of your religion. Thus the enchantment will end and my troubled soul shall rest in peace".

The timid maiden approached hesitantly, put her hand in the fountain and, collecting some water, spilled some on the pale face of the mournful apparition.

The beautiful vision smiled and, dropping her lute at Jacinta's feet, crossed her arms over her chest and faded gradually away, so that she seemed to turn into a mere shower of dew drops falling like pearls into the fountain.

Jacinta withdrew from the hall with a mixture of terror and amazement. She could barely sleep that night and, when she woke at daybreak from her disturbed sleep, it all seemed as if it had been a delirious dream. But when she went down to the hall she saw that the apparition had been real, as at the edge of the fountain lay the silver lute, glinting in the rays of the rising sun.

She sought her aunt immediately and told her all that had happened, urging her to come and see the lute as proof of the reality of her story. If the good lady harboured any doubts, they dissipated completely when Jacinta touched the instrument, as she played such breathtaking melodies that even Fredegunda's cold heart melted. What other than a supernatural melody could produce such an overwhelming effect?

The extraordinary powers of the lute became more famous day by day: whoever went by the tower would stop, enchanted, without daring to breathe, completely spell-bound. Fame of this prodigy spread far and wide; news of its marvellous powers travelled from city to city throughout Andalusia, with its inhabitants so devoted to music. No one talked of anything other than the beautiful rose of the Alhambra.

179

Meanwhile, the mood at the Spanish court was different. The monarch, Philip V, was a hopeless hypochondriac, prone to all sorts of fancies. He would sometimes stay in bed for weeks on end. There was no more effective way to calm the moods of the revered king than the power of music. The queen was therefore careful to surround herself with the most celebrated musicians and singers around. But the king's ailments persisted.

At that time, news of the renowned lute player who was gaining the whole of Andalusia's admiration also reached the court. The king's wife immediately despatched her emissaries to bring her to the court.

Only a few days later, as the queen was strolling through the palace gardens with her maids of honour, the celebrated artist from Granada was brought before her. She was accompanied by the watchful Fredegunda, who informed her majesty about the beautiful girl's history and ancestry.

"If your skill matches your renown", she told the young girl, "and you manage to banish the evil spirits possessing the sovereign, your fortune will be in my care and I will shower you with honours and wealth".

Impatient to test out her skills, she led her to the king's chamber. Jacinta followed with her eyes lowered through the crowd of guards and courtiers, until they reached an imposing but sumptuously decorated chamber hung in black tapestries. The body of the king lay in a raised coffin, as he had convinced himself he was dead and needed to be buried.

The stately dame entered the royal chamber in silence and, pointing to a footstool in a dark corner of the room, signalled the young girl to sit down there and begin. At first she touched the strings of her lute with a trembling hand, but she soon grew more confident and enthusiastic as she played. She produced such a heavenly melody that all those present could scarcely believe it came from a mere mortal. The monarch, already believing he was in the world of spirits, thought it was some melody played by angels.

The sublime artist continued to move imperceptibly between tunes, and accompanied by her instrument, began to sing an exquisite romantic ballad which celebrated the ancient glories of the Alhambra and the Moors' enterprising warfare. Her whole soul lent itself to the song, as the memory of the Alhambra was intimately joined to the story of her love.

The funereal chamber resonated with the notes of the beautiful, revitalising song, and finally managed to cheer the monarch's gloomy heart. He lifted his head and looked around. Then he sat up in his coffin and his eyes started to brighten until, eventually, he stood up and asked for his sword and clothes.

The triumph of music, of the magical lute, was complete. The demon of melancholy was expelled and it could truly be said that the dead had returned to life. The windows of the apartment were thrown open, so that the sun's rays could bathe the room with light - the room that moments before had been filled with sadness. All eyes sought the beautiful singer, but she had fainted suddenly upon catching sight of her lover Ruiz de Alarcón. He put his arms round her in time to stop her from falling...

The lovers were married in the Alhambra, in the presence of the king and queen, who came to consider the young couple as their protégés and showered them with favours and honours. Fredegunda too was happy, her withered old heart finally softening with joy for Jacinta and perhaps also because of the royal coins...

# Contents